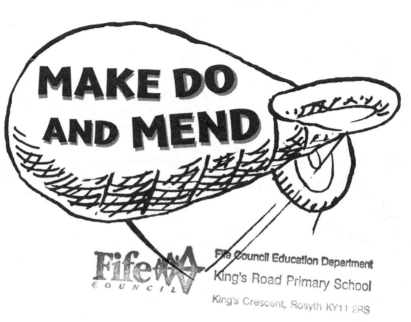

MAKE DO AND MEND

Fife **COUNCIL**

by Jack Wood
Illustrations by Tim Sell

W
FRANKLIN WATTS
LONDON • SYDNEY

First published in 2001 by Franklin Watts
96 Leonard Street, London EC2A 4XD

Text © Jack Wood 2001
Illustrations © Tim Sell 2001

The right of Jack Wood to be identified as
the Author of this Work has been asserted by
him in accordance with the Copyright, Designs
and Patents Act, 1988

Editor: Lesley Bilton
Designer: Jason Anscomb
Consultant: Anita M. Ballin, Former Head of Education,
Imperial War Museum

A CIP catalogue record for this book
is available from the British Library

ISBN 0 7496 3903 2 (hbk)
     0 7496 4010 3 (pbk)

Dewey Classification 942.084
Printed in Great Britain

MAKE DO AND MEND

by Jack Wood
Illustrations by Tim Sell

TALES OF THE SECOND WORLD WAR

Chapter 1
A Discovery

"Oh no!" groaned Roy Pitt. He stopped in his tracks so suddenly that the sledge he was dragging bumped into his heels. "Just look at this mess!"

A splintered pile of wood lay at the foot of the big oak tree that overhung the pond.

"There must have been a storm here in the park while we were away last week. Still, it means we've more wood for the fire," said Roy's sister, Heather, as she picked up a plank, dumped it on the sledge and banged her mittened hands together.

"But don't you see? It's my tree house. My den. It's been blown down," said Roy.

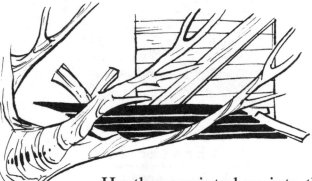

Heather squinted up into the tree's branches. The pale sun shone weakly on the remains of Roy's den. "Well, the floor and one of the walls are still there. You can rebuild it."

"You must be joking! It took me months to finish it." Roy kicked a piece of corrugated iron which had formed part of the den's roof. All winter long he'd scoured bombed-out houses in search of the very best furnishings.

His den had everything. Sandbags. A gun turret. It even boasted a Union Jack which fluttered from a flag pole.

If the Germans invaded, he was going to hole up there and see them off. Just let them try to capture him – he'd show 'em!

And now his den was in pieces because there'd been a storm in Parsons Park. Shaking his head sadly, Roy knelt down and picked up one of the nail-studded planks.

"Be careful," warned Heather, dropping another lump of wood on the sledge. "Ma said she'd wallop us if we ruin any more clothes. We've already used up all our clothing coupons for the year.* She said she's not mending your shorts if you rip them again. You'll have to go to school in your underpants."

"I don't care. I want to find my Union Jack," muttered Roy, poking about in the den's wreckage.

*Find out about clothes rationing on page 60

Heather shivered and jammed her hands further into her pockets. Snowflakes like white paper scraps had begun to fall from the dark sky. One floated close to her face and she caught it on her tongue. "It's getting late. Dad'll be cross. He told us to be home with the wood before dark. He can't light the fire until we get back. The house'll be freezing."

"I'm not going without my flag," Roy repeated. "Hey! What's this?" He stopped scrabbling, knelt back on his heels and stared at the square package he'd uncovered. "This wasn't part of my den." With gentle hands he brushed some snow off the object. "Wow! It's a parachute!"

"What?"

"A parachute."

"It can't be."

"It *is* a parachute!"

"Don't believe you."

The dark heavy material of the bundle was torn at one corner. Roy carefully wiggled a couple of his fingers in the tear, and tugged. Out snaked a length of floaty white material.

"See for yourself," he said in a pleased voice.

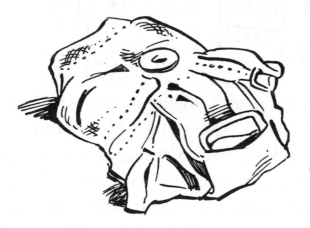

Chapter 2
Hubert's Unexpected Bath

Heather wasn't convinced. "It's an old sack," she sniffed, "filled with rubbishy bits of cloth. Parachutes are enormous."

"Only when they're open. It's a *PACKED* parachute," shouted Roy excitedly. "I saw one once at the Grubb's house. Archie Grubb brought it back with him when he came home on leave from the Air Force. He said it was a damaged one that wasn't needed." Roy paused and looked thoughtful. "There's a lot of silk in a parachute."

Heather nodded her head. "Gert Grubb's wedding dress was white and it had ever such a long train. Everybody wondered where she got the material."

She eyed the package with growing interest. "If it really *is* a parachute, I bet Ma could make us masses of clothes out it. I bet we could sell it for lots of –"

CRACK!

A loud crashing noise coming from the trees behind them made her break off and grab Roy's shoulder. "Quick! There's someone coming! Hide it! If anyone sees we'll have to hand it in to the Government or something."

Roy moved fast. He shoved the parachute deep into the bushes, and then hastily shinned up the tree, getting bark stains on the front of his shirt. But he was innocently inspecting the remains of his den by the time the intruder emerged from the woods.

It was a boy. And not just *any* boy. It was Hubert Moon from the house next door.

Hubert's fat body was swaddled in so many clothes that he looked like a well-lagged hot water tank.

His spotty face peered out from a hand-knitted woollen helmet, and a hand-knitted scarf was wrapped many times round his neck. Hand-knitted mittens poked out of the sleeves of his jacket. His knee socks (hand-knitted) were pulled high up his legs.

"What are you doing?" he quizzed in his annoying nasal voice. "I heard you shouting about a parachute. Where is it? I want to see it. You won't be allowed to keep it, you know. You'll have to give it to the authorities. You've got your shirt and jacket all dirty. My Ma says I'm not to play with you Pitts."

Roy waited until Hubert stopped for breath. "Well buzz off then, Hubert Moon. *We* don't want to play with *you* anyway."

Hubert and his nosey mother lived next door to the Pitts in Balaclava Terrace. Hubert was a fat pest and his Ma, Mrs Moon, was known to everyone in the street as Mrs Moan because she never stopped moaning.

"You're hiding it. The parachute's up there, isn't it?" Hubert persisted.

"Shut up about parachutes. We ain't got a parachute." Heather gave Hubert a level stare. "What are you doing in the park anyway? I thought you weren't allowed out in the cold. Baby!"

Hubert (according to his mother) was delicate.

"Ma says it's all right as long as I'm well wrapped-up." Hubert tucked his scarf firmly down the front of his jacket. "I'm looking for bits of aeroplane. A German bomber was shot down over the other side of the park on Friday. You don't know, because you Pitts weren't here. The wardens and rescue teams took the pieces of plane away, but there's a big black

hole left. They took the pilot away as well. I watched 'em. You didn't, because you were at a soppy wedding."

Roy gazed down at him enviously. Last week Ma had dragged the whole Pitt family to a cousin's wedding. Dad, Gran, Lenny, Joanie, Roy and Heather had been forced into their uncomfortable best clothes and made to spend several miserable days at their aunt's house helping with the celebrations.

And a German bomber had crashed in Parsons Park while they were away!

Typical!

"You're hiding a parachute up there. I heard you. I'm going to have a look." Hubert grabbed a branch and swung himself up into the tree.

The branch broke and he landed on his bottom on the hard icy ground.

He tried again, choosing a thicker branch. This one bore his weight, and slowly he huffed and puffed his way up towards Roy.

It was a long business, but Hubert was determined – despite being unfit and weighed down with heavy clothes. When he finally plonked himself down on the den floor, he was wheezing like an old steam engine.

Roy counted to ten. Then he planted a foot in the middle of Hubert's back.

And kicked.

Arms flailing, Hubert fell out of the tree. "Helllllppppp!"

Roy grinned as he waited for the despairing yell to end in a splash.

It didn't. Hubert's cry for help had been answered. His shorts had caught on a protruding branch, and he was suspended over the grey freezing water. For several thrilling seconds he hung there, then, with a slow ripping sound, the material of his shorts gave way.

"Aaargh!"

With a further high-pitched scream, Hubert resumed his interrupted journey towards the

water. Heather laughed so much she fell down by the side of the pond.

SPLOSH!

Heather soon stopped laughing. As Hubert hit the pond, a wall of muddy water flew into the air and drenched her from head to foot.

"Don't just lie there!" shouted Roy, as he slid down the tree, adding more stains to his shirt. "Scoot!"

Casting only a backward glance at Hubert (already clambering out of the water), the pair of them fled. Behind them bounced the sledge, shedding logs as it bumped over the rough snow-covered track. They didn't stop running until they reached the edge of the park.

"We'll come back tonight and pick up the parachute. It must have fallen out of that German bomber Hubert was talking about and crashed onto my tree house." Roy panted as he scrubbed at the front of his shirt. "Well, it's mine now.

The Government owes it to me. After all it was *my* den that it wrecked."

"There'll be trouble." Heather's hair was dripping, and her boots squelched. She wrung the skirt of her dress with one hand. A stream of water splashed onto the ground. "I bet Hubert tells his Ma you kicked him into the pond. She's not going to be happy."

Roy looked at the few logs left on the sledge. There wasn't going to be much of a fire at Number 46 Balaclava Terrace tonight. Then he looked down at his shirt. The scrubbing hadn't got rid of the dirt – it had spread it. He sighed, "I don't think *our* Ma's going to be very happy either."

Chapter 3
New Knickers for Old

She wasn't. In fact she was so unhappy that
she kept Roy and Heather in that evening.
They were made to sit in the coldest corner of
the icy cold room and set to work unravelling
one of Dad's old woollen jumpers.

"And when the two of you have finished
that," Ma snapped, eyeing the pile of mending
in front of her on top of the Morrison shelter,*

Morrison shelters were very sturdy – see page 61

"you can help me cut out this material." She lifted up a brightly coloured roll of red and yellow cloth, which had been buried under the holey clothes.

"How did you buy that?" Roy was puzzled. "I thought we'd used up all our clothing coupons."

"Don't ask silly questions," said Gran, looking up from her stripey knitting. She was making herself a scarf from lots of little bits of left-over wool.

"Lenny gave it to me. He bumped into a man in the Fishgutters' Arms who had some material surplus to his requirements, and –" began Ma.

"Lenny got it on the Black Market," explained Gran.

"And he asked me to keep an eye on it for him," Ma carried on.

Joanie looked up from the magazine she was reading. "And I thought it would be perfect for my new dress."

"Why do *you* get a new dress? What about me?" complained Heather.

"Because I'm going to a dance tomorrow. With an American officer. So there!"

"Well, at least he'll be able to see you in the blackout," said Dad, blowing on his hands as he walked into the room. "Brrr. It's as cold as charity in here. This fuel saving is getting ridiculous. We'll all freeze to death, then the Germans needn't bother to invade us."

He wandered over to the Morrison, picked up the bolt of cloth, held it at arm's length and blinked. "No danger of getting knocked down by a tank in the dark if you're wearing a dress made out of this. You'll look like a plate of rhubarb and custard."

Heather sniggered.

"Ha, ha. Very funny." Joanie snatched back the flowered cloth indignantly. "Magenta and primrose are extremely fashionable."

"Be quiet the lot of you," ordered Ma. "I'm trying to do something important. Let's hear those instructions again, Joanie."

Joanie turned the pages of her magazine and read out loud. *"Make Do and Mend.* Get the most out of your used clothes. Number One: how to transform those worn out lace curtains into a dashing summer jacket. Number Two: how to obtain the most out of your old corset bones. Number Three: how to make a brand new pair of knickers out of two old pairs."*

*Find out more about Making Do on page 62

"That's the one," said Ma.

"First, unpick the gussets –"

"Doing something important!" scoffed Dad. "Making bloomers!"

"It's important to me," rapped Ma. "I've not a pair of drawers left to my name. *And* there's a shortage of elastic."

Dad snorted. "Look at me." He groped under his chair, found a half-full bottle of beer, lifted it to his lips and gulped noisily. "I don't get my knickers in a twist about all the shortages *I* have to put up with, do I? There's hardly any beer – the pub ran out yesterday."

He gazed at the almost empty bottle glumly. "Only allowed five inches of water in the bath. Can't get razor blades for love nor money. No cigarettes. No lav paper. No petrol. No coal."*

"That's the worst thing," agreed Gran. "I was so cold yesterday afternoon, I put my feet in the gas oven to keep them warm."

Knock! Knock! Knock!

"Who can that be at this hour?" Ma put down the pair of knickers she was attacking with the scissors.

"Hide that material," ordered Gran. "We don't want anyone seeing that and asking questions."

Ma covered up the floral cloth with a threadbare old dressing-gown of Lenny's, while Dad lifted the blackout curtain and peered out.

*Fuel was in short supply – see page 63

"Oh no! It's Moaning Minnie from next door. And she's got that fat son with her. She looks upset about something."

Roy dropped his ball of wool.

"Told you so," said Heather.

Chapter 4
Short Shrift

Mrs Moan was squeaking with indignation as she propelled Hubert into the room.

"Ten coupons," she screamed, pointing to his shredded shorts. "I need ten clothing coupons to buy Hubert a new pair of shorts."

"Size of him it ought to be double," muttered Dad. "Anyway, what's it matter to us if your son splits his pants?"

"It was *your* son's fault," Mrs Moan pointed at Roy. "He kicked my poor delicate lambkin into Parsons Park pond, and then ran off leaving him to drown. Murderer!" She hugged Hubert protectively.

"Boys can't drown when they're that size," said Dad, tipping up his bottle and squinting sadly at the bottom. "They just float."

"What a beautiful coat you're wearing, Queenie," said Ma hastily.

Mrs Moan simpered, "I bought it yesterday from Mrs Hogg. She was given a blanket and a candlewick bedspread by the Women's Voluntary Service when her house was bombed last month. She chopped up the bedspread and made it into this coat."

"Lovely," said Ma, fingering the rough material.

"Anyway, that's got nothing to do with my Hubert's shorts." Mrs Moan shook off Ma's admiring hand. "What are you going to do about them?"

"Roy's got a spare pair for best, but," Ma looked doubtful, "I don't think they'd fit Hubert."

"You feed that boy too much," said Dad. "God knows how he gets to be that size in a time of food shortages."

Mrs Moan wasn't sidetracked. "How is he to go to school? He can't leave the house."

"Well that's a blessing. Keep him inside for the duration of the war," said Dad, cheering up. "I can't stand the sight of him and his spots. Puts me right off my food."

"Why, you –" In her indignation, Mrs Moan let go of her son's shoulder. Hubert, released from his mother's grasp, sidled over to Roy and Heather.

"I know you've got a parachute hidden up in your old tree house. And I'm going to get it. I'll pay you back for kicking me in that pond. Ma says I could have died. If I get pneumonia, I still might."

"Well hurry up and get on with it, and give us all some peace," said Roy.

Hubert opened his mouth to reply, but his voice was drowned by the ear-splitting wail of the air-raid siren.

The Pitts groaned.

"Not again. We had an alert last night."

"And that was a false alarm."

"I'm not going outside to that freezing cold air-raid shelter," said Gran. "If I'm going to be bombed, I'd rather be in a warm bed." She stabbed her knitting needles into her scarf, hauled herself out of her chair and clumped out of the door.

"Well, I'm not taking any chances. Into the Morrison with you two," said Ma. She bit her thread and folded up the hacked pieces of knickers. Then she let down the side of the Morrison shelter.

"Never mind the air raid!" Mrs Moan stuck to her guns. "What about Hubert's shorts? You owe me ten coupons!"

"We've told you. We haven't any coupons and there's not a scrap of material in the house," Ma explained patiently as she scooped up the holey shirts and Lenny's old dressing gown.

Mrs Moan pounced on the now uncovered bolt of cloth. "What do you call this then?" she cried, brandishing the bolt of flowery material triumphantly.

Chapter 5
Lenny Gets Some Coal

"At last!" said Ma, sinking into a chair as the front door slammed behind Mrs Moan. "I thought she'd never go."

"How could you give her that material?" wailed Joanie. "It was going to be for my dress. Now it's wasted on that horrid boy."

"I had to shut her up somehow," Ma apologised. "*But*," she glared at Roy, "it wouldn't have been necessary if a certain person hadn't kicked Hubert into the pond in the first place. What on earth possessed you?"

"I was protecting something. Something for us. Something that you'll –"

SLAM!

The door opened and the entry of his older brother, Lenny, prevented Roy from telling Ma about the parachute. Lenny was filthy.

"Not another one!" Ma folded her arms. "And what have *you* been doing to get into that state? And why have you been walking the streets during an alert?"

"It was only a stray plane," said Lenny,

brushing his coat. Showers of black dust landed on the already dirty carpet. "Just a Jerry unloading a few bombs on his way back home. I sheltered in the doorway of the bank. I thought if it got a direct hit I'd be surrounded by money."

"And were you?" asked Ma. "The bomb must have been close. You're covered with dirt from the blast."

"No, the bombs landed miles away, worse luck. The ack-ack battery tried to shoot the plane down, but they missed by miles. They're still congratulating themselves over that one they shot down in the park last week. You'd think they'd won the war single-handed."

"Well, if you weren't bombed," said Ma, "why are you so dirty?" She stepped closer to Lenny and wrinkled her nose. "And what's that awful smell?"

"I've been helping Nutty Slack on his rounds."

"You've been helping the coal man with his deliveries? Since when have you done an honest day's work?"

"Ha!" Lenny winked at Dad. "Who said anything about work? I was collecting manure from old Nutty's horse, Pegasus. People are paying good money for quality horse dung to

spread on their allotments. Makes the cabbages grow. I got five bucket loads."

"Well, you pong! You'd better go and change."

"*And* I did a deal with old Nutty. He's slipped me a couple of sacks of coal."

"Good lad," said Dad rubbing his hands. "That's the best news I've heard this winter. Have you hidden them somewhere safe? That pesky warden is always running in and out of the house pretending to inspect the blackout."

Dad didn't like Boggy Marsh, their local Air-Raid Precautions warden. He took his duties very seriously and suspected the Pitts of half the wrong-doing in his area.

He was usually right.

"Don't worry," said Lenny. "I've hidden the sacks in the outside lav."

"How much did you pay?" asked Dad.

"Nothing. It's a fair trade." Lenny grinned. "Nutty's wife wants a new dress, so I've promised him that material I left here earlier. Hand it over, Ma. Nutty's waiting outside."

The room went silent.

"Oh dear," said Heather.

Chapter 6
Cold Comfort

The house was still freezing. Nutty had left in a huff, taking his two bags of coal with him.

"I don't care if it is like the North Pole in here. Off with those smelly clothes!" Ma stood over Lenny sternly. "And don't think I've finished with you two either," she added, swinging round to Roy and Heather. "Back in the Morrison! The All Clear's not gone yet."

Roy and Heather had been trying to make a sneaky exit from the shelter.

"It's a good job tomorrow's Monday. You can both lend a hand with the wash – after all, you make most of the work," said Ma as she pulled off Lenny's dirty mac.

"Do we have to, Ma?" groaned Heather. "I hate wash day."

"Well why did you get so mucky?"

"And why did you have to push that fat idiot from next door into the pond?" Joanie was still brooding over the loss of her dress.

"I was only trying to stop him pinching my parachute," said Roy.

"A parachute?" Lenny froze, one leg out of his trousers.

"Did you say a parachute?" Dad choked on his beer.

"Yeh. I found one. In the park. It'd knocked down my tree house and –"

"We think it must have fallen out of that German plane that was shot down last week," put in Heather.

Lenny rubbed his chin. "We-ell, I suppose it could have come adrift. German pilots sometimes keep their parachutes under their seats to save space in the cockpit. So when he was shot down, the parachute might have fallen free of the rest of the wreckage."

"I thought we could use it to make clothes. Ma's done nothing but moan about not having any knickers for weeks, and there's lots of silk in a parachute."

"Remember Gert Grubb's wedding dress," added Heather.

"I could get a lot of money for a parachute," said Lenny.

Dad rubbed his hands. "Now where did you leave it?"

"One parachute could make a dozen wedding dresses," said Joanie dreamily.

"Or a hundred pairs of knickers," Ma's voice trembled with longing.

"Shut up about knickers," ordered Dad. "I'm trying to get to the bottom of this. Now pay attention Roy. Where is it?"

"Where's what?" asked Roy.

"The parachute!"

"We found it by the pond in the park," said Heather quickly.

"It had ruined my tree house . . ."

"Then Hubert came, so we hid it . . ."

"We were going to go back tonight, but Ma wouldn't let us go out . . ."

"She will now," said Lenny, clambering back into his trousers. "Come on Roy, let's get going. We'll have that parachute back here in a jiffy."

"No," said Ma firmly. "No one is going out when the alert is on. It'll still be there tomorrow. Parachutes don't have legs. Now off with those mucky trousers, Lenny."

Lenny muttered under his breath, but he obeyed Ma.

So did everyone else. Roy crawled back into the Morrison shelter alongside Heather and wrapped his blanket round him. Tomorrow he'd get up very early and be in the park before breakfast.

Chapter 7

Dirty Work

But it was mid-morning before Roy left home to pick up the parachute.

He'd pleaded and pleaded but Ma had carried out her threat, and made him spend hours helping her with the Monday wash. Heather was still pegging out clothes.

There'd been a heavy overnight frost and the path was icy. Roy had almost reached the pond when he heard the sound of voices and heavy feet crunching on the path behind him.

Diving into the bushes, he kept his head down. The voices came closer.

"Quite right, my boy. Quite right. If there is a parachute, it belongs to the Government. It's not for any Tom, Dick or Harry to make off with. Those Pitts are behind most of the trouble in this neighbourhood."

It was Warden Marsh – no other voice in the district was as loud as that.

"Will there be a reward?" A second voice shrilled through the still air.

 Two figures came into view. The first was Hubert – unmissable in his new floral shorts. The traitor! This was what he'd meant about getting even. He'd tattled to Boggy Marsh about the parachute.

"Only the reward of knowing that you've done your duty. Is this the place?"

Parting the frosty twigs with his fingers, Roy watched in frustration. A couple more steps and they'd be on top of the bushes hiding his parachute!

"That's it," Hubert squeaked. "It must be there in the tree. When I climbed up yesterday I was getting close. That's why Roy Pitt kicked me in the pond. My Ma says I could have died. She says I still might. She says –"

Warden Marsh wasn't interested in Hubert's possible death.

"We need to get it down." The warden ran his eyes up the tree. "There's no way I could get up there." He gnawed his lip and gave Hubert a calculating stare. "Look here, boy. Just shin up that tree and throw it down."

"Me?" squealed Hubert. "What about my new shorts? My Ma will kill me if they get ripped."

"Never mind your Ma. You'll be doing an important service for your country."

Roy shifted unhappily. Would Warden Marsh search the bushes when no parachute was discovered in the den?

Twigs snapped close to him and he swung round. It was Heather! She squirmed through the bushes until she was crouched next to him.

"Why didn't you wait for me? Look at Hubert climbing. He'll get stuck," she giggled.

Roy didn't see the joke. "It's not funny. They might find my parachute."

Loud puffs and groans accompanied Hubert's slow progress up the tree.

"Yes, that's right, boy. That's it. Like a sack. Throw it down."

"OK. Here it comes!"

"Aaaargh!"

A sack-like bundle whizzed through the air and landed with a thump on the top of Warden Marsh's head.

It split open and a cloud of black soot rose to the heavens.

Roy was transfixed. "That's not my parachute!"

"Of course it's not, silly." Heather gave a knowing smirk. "Lenny picked it up early this morning. He wasn't going to risk losing something valuable. I saw him hide it in Gran's hen-house. The noise of the chickens woke me up, so I went out into the garden. Lenny said he thought Hubert would tell Warden Marsh about the parachute, and they'd be along for it, so he left one of Nutty Slack's

soot sacks in the tree. Just to give them something to think about."

"You could have told me," said Roy.

Heather sniggered. "I thought it would be funnier not to. Look at Boggy."

Warden Marsh was trying to sit up, but he couldn't see for soot.

"Help!" A wail came from above.

Their eyes were torn from the warden to Hubert. He'd hurled the sack with too much enthusiasm, and was now struggling to keep his balance. For a moment he teetered on the base of the tree house. Then he fell.

And landed on top of Warden Marsh.

"WOOMPH!"

All the breath was expelled from the warden's body. A dense cloud of soot rose into the air for the second time and enveloped both of them.

Hubert was the first to recover. But then, his fall had been cushioned by Warden Marsh's stomach.

Boggy lay gasping on the ground, looking like a whale washed up on a beach. He tried to say something, but all that came out of his mouth was a lot of black powder. He tried again, and this time he managed a threatening croak: "If this is your idea of a joke, boy, then you're going to pay for it."

Hubert said nothing. Then he looked down at his filthy clothes. The new shorts that his Ma had spent hours making were covered with soot. His lower lip began to tremble.

Heather tapped Roy on the shoulder, and jerked her head. He nodded and they both crept away from the sound of Boggy's shouts.

"Hubert's ever so dirty," gloated Heather. "I bet he'll catch it from his Ma."

"If he escapes Warden Marsh," said Roy, jerking Heather behind a tree as Hubert whizzed past them, the ground shaking beneath his flat feet. "I never realised that Hubert could run so fast."

"Come on." Heather brushed some twigs from her coat. "Let's go home and see how they're getting on with that parachute."

"*My* parachute," said Roy.

Chapter 8
Roy's Reward

The main room of Number 46 Balaclava
Terrace was packed with bustling people. A
crackling fire, piled high with coal, kept the
workers warm.

Gran, Ma and Joanie were measuring,
cutting and sewing large pieces of the
parachute silk.

"Pass the elastic."

"After you with the scissors."

"Let's have another look at that pattern."

It was six in the evening and the Pitt family had been toiling over the parachute silk all afternoon.

Lenny looked up from a sheet of paper covered with scribbles. "Right. This is how it breaks down. First, there's material for Nutty's wife. She's paid with two bags of coal. Then there's material for a dress for Joanie. Material for a dress for Heather. Material for a dozen pairs of bloomers for Ma. The remainder of the silk I'm selling to Sid Shorthouse. He's going to make it up into knickers at his factory and flog 'em for two shillings a pair. And he's paying us. . ." Lenny went back to his piece of paper and checked the figures. "The bottom line is that we make five pounds!"

Dad whistled.

"What about me?" said Roy. "*I'm* the one who found the parachute. *I'm* the one whose den was wrecked. I should get something too."

"That's true," said Dad. "Give him five bob, Lenny. And Roy, you can show your gratitude by bringing in some more coal."

Lenny dug in his pocket and flipped two large silver coins to Roy, who caught them, picked up the coal scuttle, and left the room.

He was filling the scuttle with coal from the sack in the outside lav when he heard a high wailing noise coming from the garden next door. Stacking some sandbags against the fence, Roy climbed up and looked into the Moans' back garden.

"And when I've finished this washing, I'm going to have some very severe words with you, young man. Rolling about in soot! You're no better than those Pitts next door!"

Mrs Moan was hanging out clothes on the line. Hubert's jacket, pullover, shirt, socks, scarf and underclothes were pegged out to dry. Hubert himself was standing in the kitchen doorway dressed in nothing but an old blanket.

"But I didn't do anything."

"Then why are your clothes ruined?"

"I was only trying to help my country."

"A likely story." Mrs Moan stabbed the last peg into place, and swept back into the house, grabbing Hubert by the scruff of the neck as she passed.

"It was all Roy Pitt's fault. I might get pneumonia. I might die. I might –"

The slam of the kitchen door cut off Hubert's lamentations.

Jingling the coins in his pocket, Roy grinned, picked up the full coal scuttle and headed back into his warm house.

Tomorrow he'd start rebuilding his den.

NOTES

Clothes Rationing

Clothes rationing was introduced in June 1941. The aim of the scheme was to release the people who worked in the clothing industry to allow them do more useful war work.

Each person in the country was given an allowance of coupons and each item of clothing was worth a certain number of coupons. Early in 1942, every man, woman and child was allocated sixty coupons, and these had to last them for fifteen months.

Twenty-six coupons were needed to obtain a man's suit, and a woman's woollen dress required eleven. For one coupon you could get two handkerchiefs. As the war went on people's clothes wore out and everyone became shabbier and shabbier.

Morrison Shelters

The Morrison shelter was named after Herbert Morrison, the Minister for Home Security. It was a large box with a steel plate top and was kept inside the house. Many people used it as a table during the day, and games such as table tennis were played on its top. The sides could be let down, and during air raids people sheltered inside it. Morrison shelters were very strong and some even proved capable of withstanding the collapse of a two-storey house.

Make Do and Mend

The Government used posters with slogans such as "Make Do and Mend" to persuade people to repair their clothes instead of throwing them away. They urged mothers to cut down cast-off adult clothes to make clothes for their children. One leaflet suggested making babies' bibs out of chopped-up bits of old raincoats. Another advised saving on coupons for gloves by making mittens from old bits of unravelled wool.

Fuel Rationing

It was very important for the armed forces to have fuel for their lorrys, tanks, battleships and planes. To avoid precious oil and petrol being wasted on non-military uses, the Government introduced petrol rationing. The monthly ration was so small it could easily be used up in a day. Doctors and people who needed a car for their jobs were given extra rations.

After 1942, no petrol was allowed for private cars at all. A few people adapted their cars to run on gas, but this was bulky and the adapted cars were very difficult to drive safely.

Gas and electricity were never rationed but people were told to limit their use of coal, gas, electricity, paraffin and hot water.

The Pitt Family

Gran

Dad

Joanie

Lenny

Ma

Heather

Roy

Find out more about how the Pitts survived the Second World War.

Digging for Victory 0 7496 3866 4 (Hbk)   0 7496 3960 1 (Pbk)

Spam! Whale meat! Boiled nettles! More Spam! The Pitts have had enough of food
rationing. Then Lenny finds a crate of tinned fruit . . .

Put That Light Out! 0 7496 3867 2 (Hbk)   0 7496 3961 X (Pbk)

Dad's fallen down a bomb crater! Lenny's walked into a lamp post! The Pitt family is
having trouble in the blackout. Then the air-raid siren goes off . . .

Careless Talk 0 7496 3902 4 (Hbk)   0 7496 4009 X (Pbk)

A newcomer has moved into Balaclava Terrace. He never speaks, and he always
clutches a briefcase! Is he a German spy? The Pitt family set out to investigate.